Small but Mighty

Written by

ALYSSA VEECH

Illustrated by

PENNY WEBER

Dedication

To my husband, for encouraging me to put
pen to paper and share my passion.

To my mother, for her advice, her love,
and her unconditional support in writing this book.

To the incredible NICU staff at Sisters of Charity
Hospital, for the wonderful care they provide
to the tiniest of patients.

With you in my belly, my love for you grew.
You know my heartbeat from the inside.

Patiently waiting for you to arrive,
a tiny miracle born before you were due.

With lungs very new,
a machine helps you breathe.
Your sweet, little cry is kept quiet.

Doctors listen to your lungs,
every day making changes.
As you grow, I whisper,
"be brave, little one."

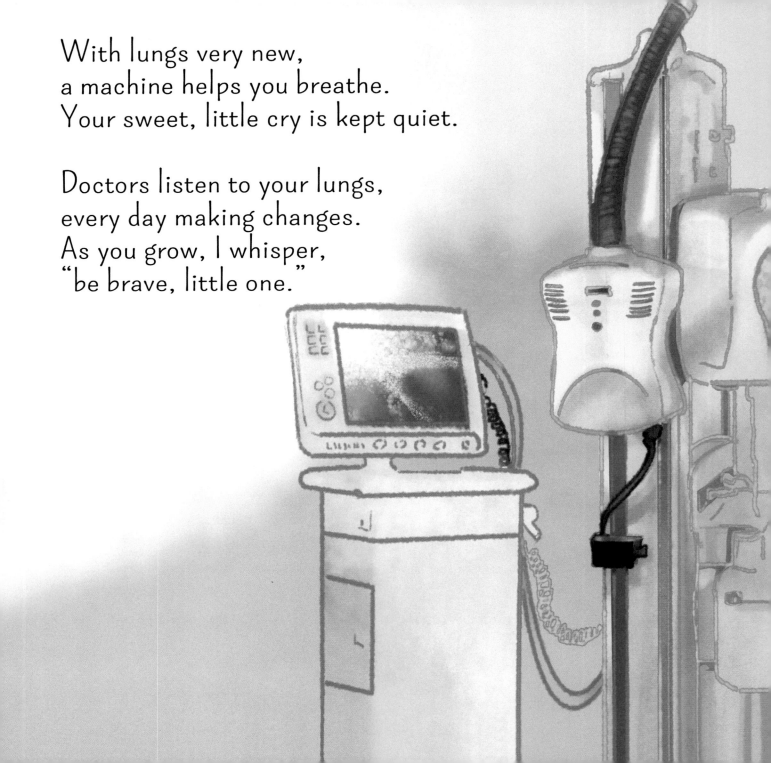

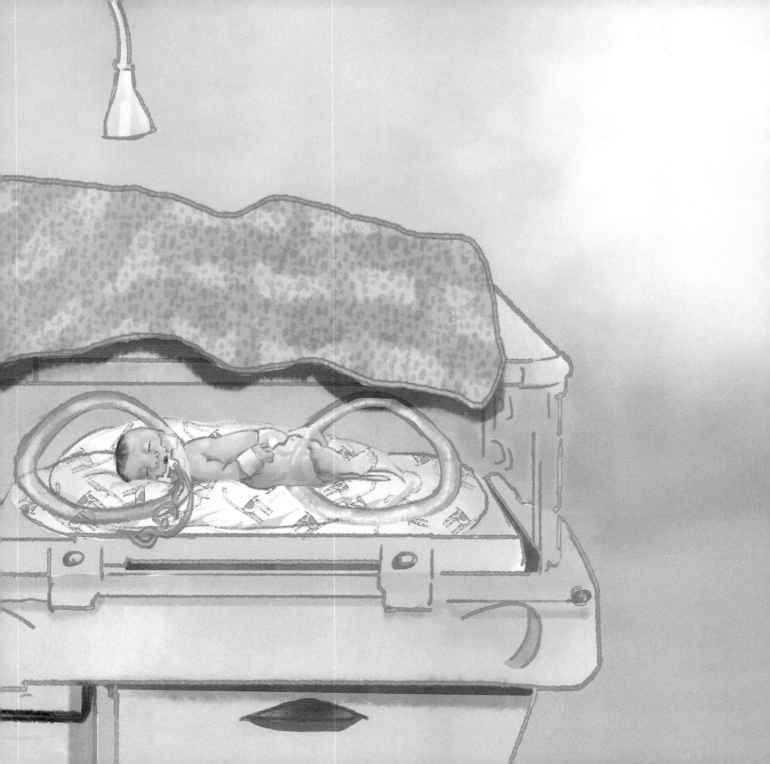

Too fragile to be held, you're warm in the isolette.
I soak you in -
your smooth skin, the wrinkles of your toes.

Sharing soft-spoken words
with the lights dimmed low.
This journey together will never be forgotten.

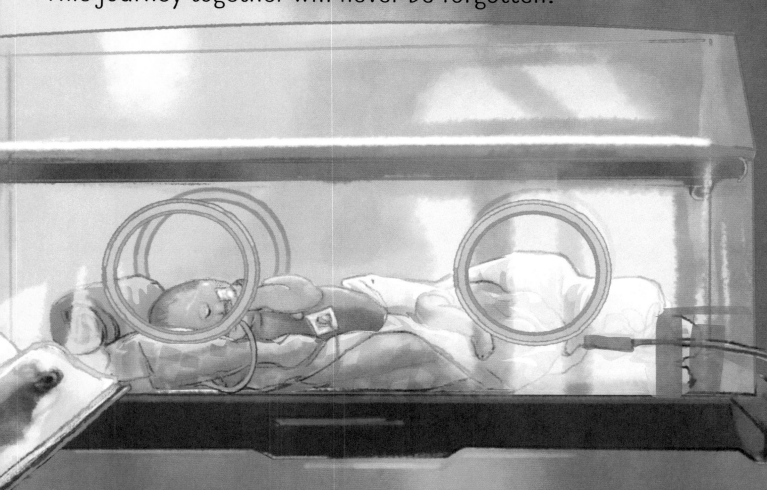

With your preemie belly, feedings start slow.
Gavage tubes and IV fluids help you stay strong.

Pumping milk around the clock, I feel close to you.
Every day, it's exciting to hear how you've grown!

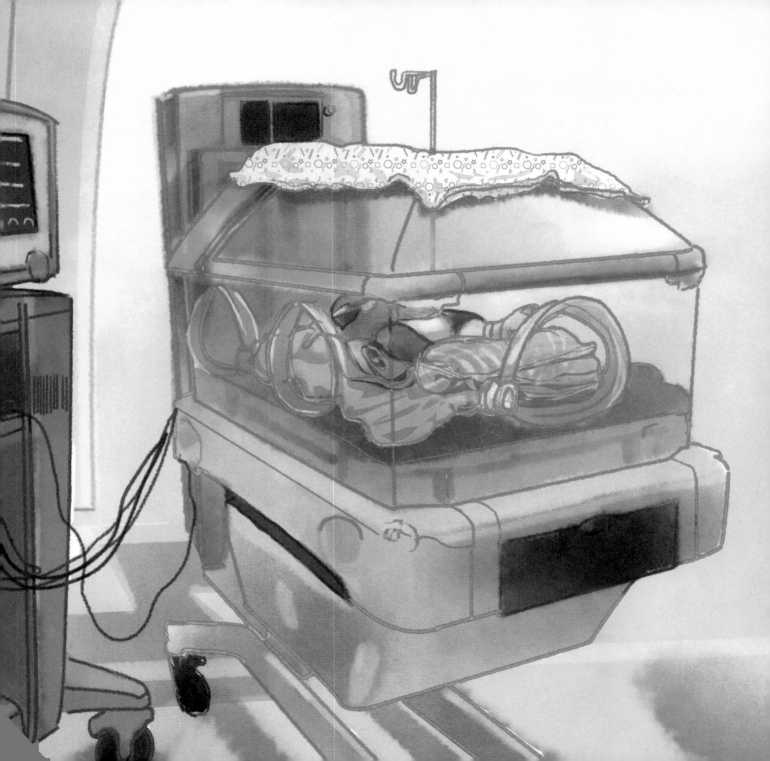

Too small to be swaddled,
my skin keeps you warm.
You sleep soundly on my chest as I watch you dream.

Your heart beats, brave and bold,
teaching unconditional love in the slightest of moments.

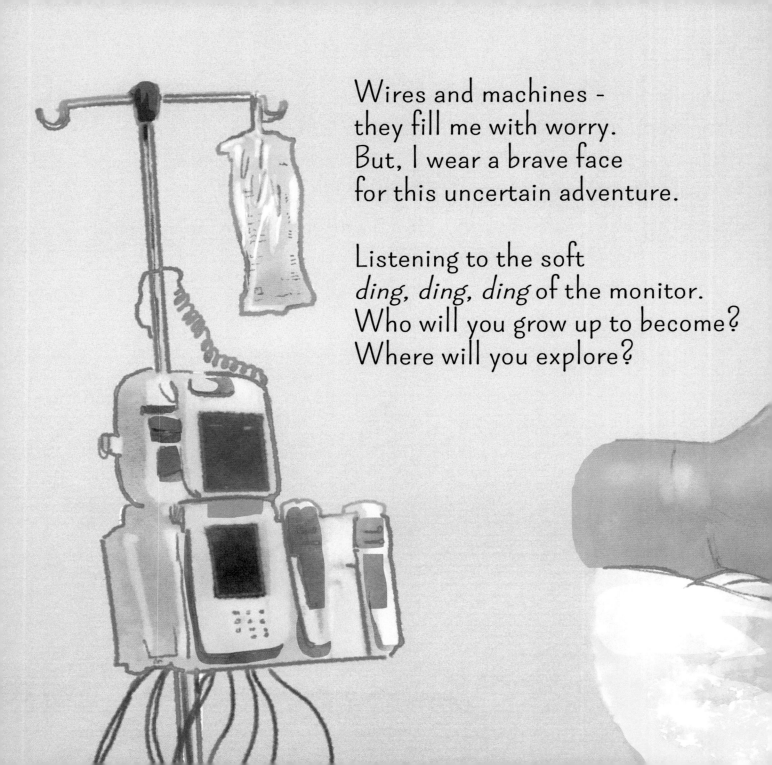

Wires and machines -
they fill me with worry.
But, I wear a brave face
for this uncertain adventure.

Listening to the soft
ding, ding, ding of the monitor.
Who will you grow up to become?
Where will you explore?

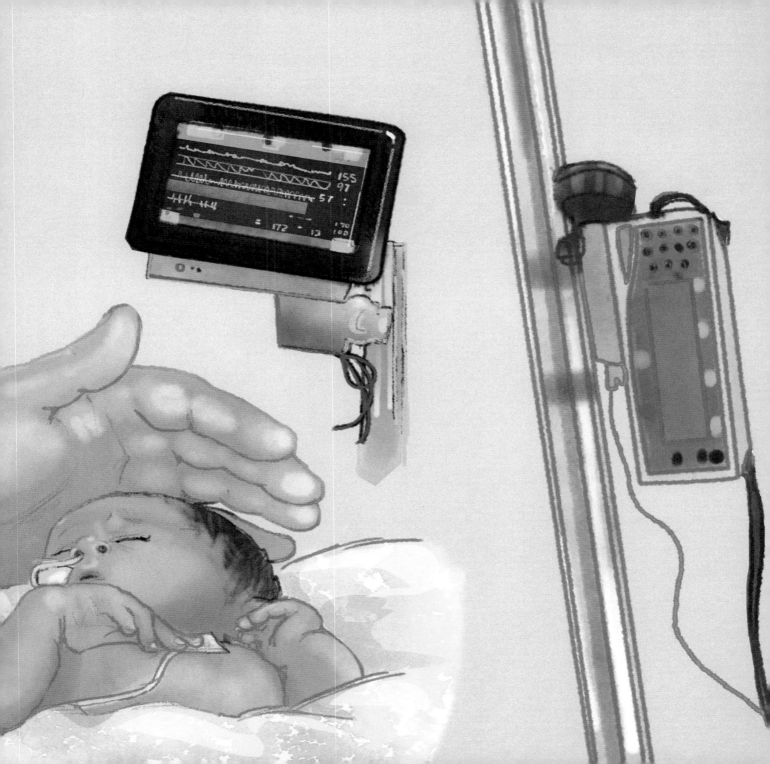

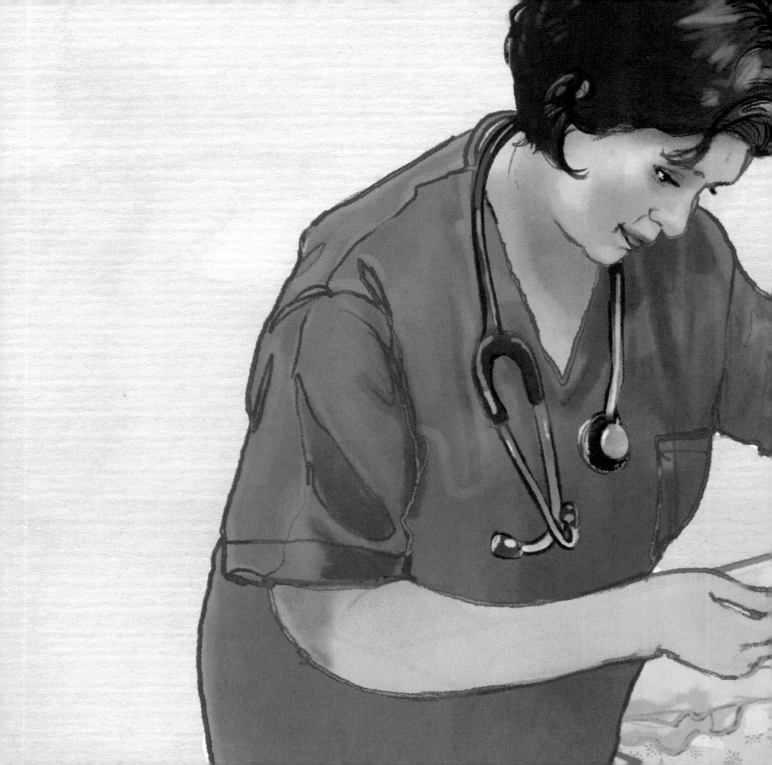

Nurses wrap you in love when I can't be there.
Warriors of hope, who fight alongside you.

They comfort and feed, change diapers and cuddle,
reminding me that there are brighter days ahead.

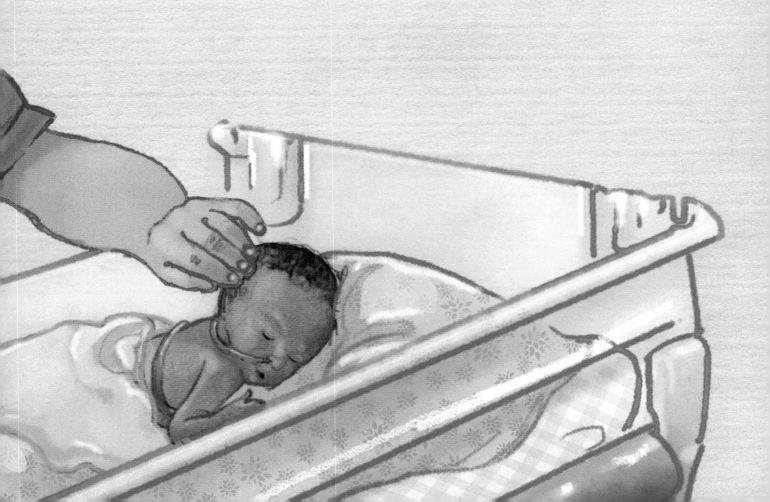

The wires and tubes - they will soon disappear.
I will dress you and hold you,
swaddled close to my heart.

With each milestone comes celebration and joy!
Working hard, every day, fighting to live.

The sadness, the love,
the fear and delight -
from small beginnings
come great things.

A precious gift
in this uncertain world.
You are small,
but you are mighty.

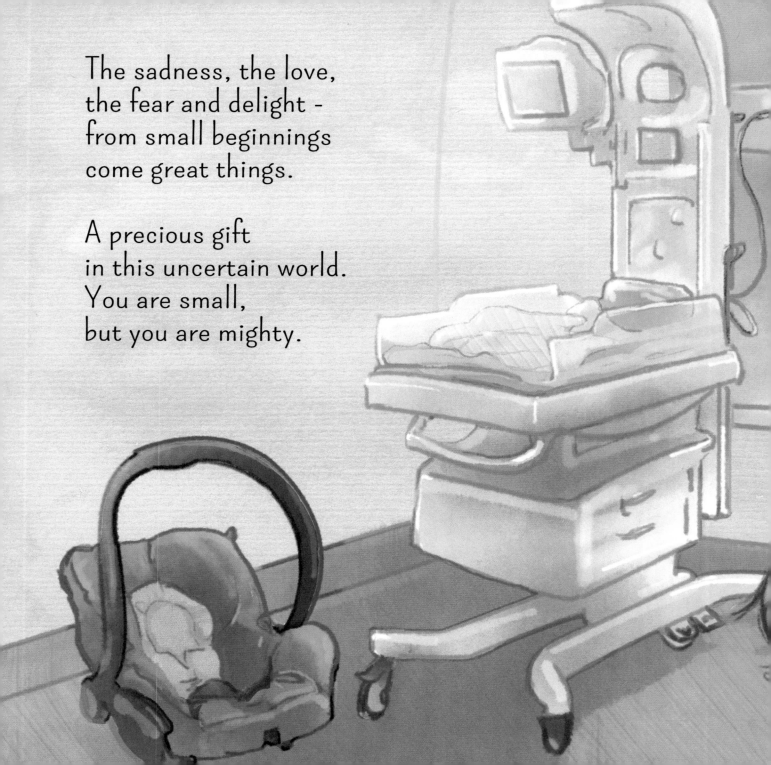

Alyssa Veech is a Neonatal Nurse Practitioner from Buffalo, New York. After obtaining a degree in nursing, she began working as a critical care nurse in the Neonatal Intensive Care Unit. Her passion for preemies led her to become a Neonatal Nurse Practitioner, earning her doctoral degree from the University of Pittsburgh.

Alyssa lives with her husband, Peter, and their dog, Sophi. She works as a Neonatal Nurse Practitioner at Sisters of Charity Hospital and is a faculty member at the University at Buffalo. In her spare time, Alyssa loves to travel and spend time with her husband and family.